Benjie

BY JOAN M. LEXAU

Benjie

ILLUSTRATED BY DON BOLOGNESE

THE DIAL PRESS NEW YORK

For Jeanne V.

"Well, Benjie, are you going to sleep all day long?" Granny called.

Benjie opened his eyes and remembered. It was Sunday, so he couldn't sleep late. He sat up and looked out the window to see what kind of a day it was.

Mrs. Atkins was leaning out the window across the courtyard from him. She was putting her bedclothes on the window sill to air them. "Hello, Benjie," she called.

Benjie looked away and pretended not to hear. He didn't like to talk to people. He didn't know why, but he just didn't.

"Go and get washed," Granny told him.

"Do I have to?" Benjie asked. He didn't wait for an answer. He knew the answer. Granny had scrubbed him and scrubbed him last night. But still he had to wash some more as soon as he woke up.

Benjie peeked out into the hallway. There was nobody there for him to have to talk to. He ran down the hall to the washroom, and then he ran back to the room where he and Granny lived.

He hurried into his Sunday clothes and got out his brown crayon and colored up the scuffs on his shoes.

At last they were all ready except for Granny's earrings. She always put them on just before they set out for church. She fixed them on now, and they jiggled and joggled as she moved and seemed to catch on fire when the light hit them.

"There, now, Benjie," Granny said, looking in the mirror, "aren't I the prettiest lady you ever saw in your life?"

"You sure are, Granny," Benjie said.

They set off, down the stairs and down the stairs and down the stairs, from the fourth floor to the sidewalk.

Mr. Atkins and some other neighbors were sitting on the stoop. They said hello to Granny. Mr. Atkins said, "Where is Benjie? I thought I saw him with you."

"Oh, he's around me somewhere," Granny said. "That boy is the shyest boy I ever saw."

As they walked down the street Granny said, "Benjie, you're going to school in a few weeks. Do you think Granny's going to school every day with you to do your talking for you? I can't sit in those little chairs they use, Benjie. I'd sit in one of those chairs and it would bust to pieces and I'd be on the floor."

They both started laughing at that and Granny forgot about scolding.

In church Granny said, "Sit up straight, Benjie." "Don't kick your heels, Benjie." "Benjie, stop that wiggling." She never yelled in church. She just whispered right in Benjie's ear, and that was worse.

After church they stopped at the bakery as they always did. Benjie liked to look at all the things in the cases, but every Sunday he wanted the same thing, a black-and-white cookie, a huge cookie, frosted half with chocolate and half with vanilla. He watched the bakery lady pick up his cookie with a piece of paper and put it in a bag. Then she picked up an apple turnover the same way for Granny and put it in the bag. She frowned because they were buying so little. Benjie liked the bakery and the bakery smell, but he was afraid of the bakery lady.

So far the day had been like every other Sunday. It was when they were nearly home that the different thing, the awful thing, happened.

Suddenly Granny stopped walking and put her hand up to her ear. "My earring!" she screamed. "Benjie, I lost my earring!"

Sure enough, Granny had only one earring on. The other earring was gone. Benjie's granddaddy had given those earrings to Granny the day they were married. Benjie didn't remember his granddaddy, but Granny talked about him a lot and about the old days so long ago.

Now after all these years one of the earrings was lost. The last Granny remembered feeling them both bobbing on her ears was when they left the church. They went back the way they had come, searching the sidewalk for the earring.

Finally Granny straightened up and said, "I don't see how we're ever going to find it, Benjie. That earring could be anywhere. Maybe somebody found it by now and took it away."

"But, Granny, we have to find it," Benjie said. Granny looked so disappointed that Benjie was ready to cry.

Granny said, "Now, look, Benjie, haven't I had the joy of those ear-rings all this time? And I've still got one to look at and remember. Maybe the good Lord did this as a lesson to me for setting such store on trinkets. You and I won't waste any tears crying over it. We'll just go on home."

NORTH SCHOOL LIBRARY
HILLSBOROUGH CITY SCHOOL DISTRICT
543 EUCALYPTUS AVENUE
HILLSBOROUGH, CALIFORNIA

They went home, and after they ate the cookie and the turnover, Granny decided to take her afternoon nap before dinner instead of after. "You just play quietly for a while and keep your good clothes clean," she told Benjie.

Instead of playing, Benjie sat on the floor and thought. Why would the Lord want to lesson Granny on those earrings, he wondered. Or did He? Granny had just said maybe. But maybe they just hadn't looked long enough. What they ought to do was go look some more.

Benjie started to tell Granny so, but she was already asleep and he decided not to say anything. Then he had a better idea. Why shouldn't he go out on his own? He wouldn't have to talk to anybody to look for an earring. He started out quickly before he could change his mind. Noiselessly he went out the door and closed it gently behind him.

When he got downstairs, there was Mr. Atkins sitting on the stoop again. Benjie tried to get around him before he could be seen, but it didn't work. Mr. Atkins stood up in his path and said, "Why, hello there, Benjie."

Benjie looked around for somewhere to hide.

"Come on, now, say hello to me just this once," Mr. Atkins said. "You might find out it isn't so hard."

Benjie opened his mouth and tried, but nothing came out.

"I see your lips moving, but I don't hear anything," Mr. Atkins said.

Benjie tried again, but only the tiniest whisper came out.

"Well, that's a start," Mr. Atkins said. "Try it once more."

Benjie took a deep breath and opened his mouth wide and hollered, "HELLO HELLO HELLO!" He put his hands over his ears to shut out the sound. He'd never made such a racket in his life. He streaked around Mr. Atkins and down to the corner where Granny had first missed her earring.

He waited on the corner until some people came along so he could cross the street with them. On the other side he walked down the sidewalk, looking first on one side and then the other, keeping his eyes glued to the ground. All of a sudden he bumped into somebody. He waited, holding his breath, to get yelled at, but nothing happened.

"I'm sorry," he whispered, and looked up.

It was a lamppost he'd bumped into. He giggled and looked around to see if anyone had seen him. Nobody had.

Benjie went on searching, looking at every inch of the sidewalk all the way to the church. There was no sign of an earring. Somebody must have found it, as Granny said.

He turned around and slowly began walking home.

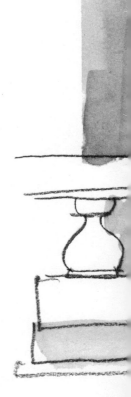

When he reached the bakery, he slowed down even more to smell the good smells. Then he remembered. Neither he nor Granny had thought of searching for the earring in here.

Benjie peeked in the doorway to see what the bakery lady was doing. She was busy putting things on shelves, so he tiptoed in and began looking around on the floor. If he was lucky, he could find the earring and be out of there without having to talk to her.

Just then she turned around and saw him. "What are you up to?" she asked.

Benjie thought of running, but then he'd never know if the earring was here. He stared down at his shoes and said, "I have to find Granny's earring."

The bakery lady had to bend down to hear him. "You won't find it here," she said crossly. "This floor's just been swept and no earring was found. Now, run along and don't bother me."

Some customers came in and she busied herself with waiting on them.

Benjie looked around the floor just in case. Then he got to thinking. What if the earring had been on the floor and been swept up? He hated to stay here any longer, but it would be awful if he was this close to it and didn't find it. There wasn't anything in sight to put sweepings in. He looked toward the back room. Did he dare go look there? The bakery lady wasn't watching, so he hurried into the back room. It was dark and hard to see at first. Finally he found a trash barrel in a corner. By climbing up on a shelf, he was able to look down into it, but it was too dark to see anything. There was a light cord above him, and he was able to reach it by standing on the rim of the trash barrel. Now he'd be able to see the earring if the light hit it. The trouble was, every time he leaned over to look in, he blocked out the light.

Then he heard footsteps coming toward him. There wasn't time to climb up and turn out the light. He hid behind the barrel.

"I thought I turned out this light," he heard the bakery lady say. "No sense wasting electricity."

Then there was a silence.

"Now, what is that little shoe doing down there!" she exclaimed. "I do believe there's a foot in it. Yes, there is. Now, you just come out from behind there. You know what I do about boys trying to steal my cakes? I call the police, that's what I do."

"I wasn't stealing your cakes," Benjie said. "I was looking for Granny's earring. And I'm going to find it, too. It's her earring, it isn't yours." Benjie's voice was shaky, but he was almost yelling.

"Just what is so important about that earring?" the bakery lady demanded. "I've lost earrings myself and never made such a fuss about it."

Benjie wanted more than ever to run home now, but he thought of how happy Granny would be to have her earring back and he made himself stay. He told the bakery lady about his granddaddy and how Granny wore the earrings every Sunday. The more he talked, the easier it was to go on talking.

When he finished, the bakery lady stopped frowning at him. "Why didn't you say they were so special in the first place?" she said.

She spread a newspaper out on the floor, and together they tipped the trash barrel on its side. She made Benjie put on a long white apron to protect his Sunday clothes.

"You go through it a little at a time," she said. Then she had to go out to wait on a customer.

Benjie emptied out the barrel little by little. Once he saw something shiny and thought he had found the earring, but it turned out to be a piece of aluminum foil.

Just when he had decided it wasn't in the barrel, there it was sparkling in his hand.

Carefully he put the dirt and the newspaper in the barrel. He didn't want the bakery lady to say he had left a mess.

The bakery lady took the earring from him and wrapped it in a piece of paper. She put the paper in a bag. "Now you won't lose it on the way home," she said.

The bag was too heavy for just an earring. Benjie looked inside and saw a cupcake.

"Thank you," he said. "Thanks a lot."

Benjie hurried home. Mr. Atkins was still sitting on the stoop, half-asleep.

Benjie tiptoed up to him. "Hello, Mr. Atkins," he yelled.

Mr. Atkins jumped up and burst out laughing. "Who is this?" he said. "It can't be Benjie!"

Benjie ran up all the steps and into his apartment.

"Where on earth have you been?" Granny said. "I was just going out to look for you."

Benjie said quickly, "Say, Granny, I found that old earring you thought you lost."

He put the earring in her hand and told her how he had found it and that he hadn't let anybody stop him from finding that earring.

Granny put both earrings on her ears and looked in the mirror. She turned her head this way and that to see the earrings sparkle in the light.

Then she hugged Benjie. "My, I'm proud of you," she said. "But do you know what? The earring wasn't the only thing lost today."

"What else was lost?" Benjie asked.

"Why, just this morning," Granny said, "I had a grandson named Benjie, just like you. But he was the most bashful boy. He hated to speak to anybody. Now he's gone. He absolutely disappeared. What do you suppose happened to him?"

"I could go out and look for him," Benjie said. He went to the door and opened it, turning his face away so Granny wouldn't see him laughing.

"You stay here," Granny said. "You're such a good finder, you just might find him. Let's get dinner ready instead."

18463